MORROW JUNIOR BOOKS
NEW YORK

Watercolors were used for the full-color illustrations.
The text type is 18-point Weiss.

Printed in the United States of America.

2 3 4 5 6 7 8 9 10

Library of Congress Cataloging-in-Publication Data
Hague, Michael.
The perfect present/Michael Hague.
p. cm.
Summary: After choosing a special gift for his sweetheart, Jack chases it all the way to her house just in time for her Christmas party.
ISBN 0-688-10880-6
[1. Gifts—Fiction. 2. Rabbits—Fiction. 3. Kangaroos—Fiction. 4. Toys—Fiction. 5. Christmas—Fiction.] I. Title.
PZ7.H12465Pe 1996 [E]—dc20 95-52427 CIP AC

To Kasha

There were toys on the counters and toys on the floor—there were even toys hanging from the ceiling.

left home to buy the perfect present.

It was Christmas Eve and Jack had not yet found a gift for his sweetheart. So he put on his favorite red coat and

Big Bear's Toy Shoppe
was filled with toys
of every shape and size.

Then Jack found it, the perfect present:
a small brown kangaroo with soft fur
and a playful smile.

Jack asked Big Bear for help.
He wanted something special,
something Ginger would love.

Big Bear placed the kangaroo in a box. He was about to close the lid when—*boing!*—out sprang the kangaroo! Hip, hop, hop...

Shoppers filled the streets,
hurrying and scurrying everywhere.

"My perfect present!" cried Jack as he ran after the toy.

The kangaroo hopped through the crowd with ease, but no matter how hard Jack tried, he could not catch that bouncing toy.

Jack couldn't see the perfect present anywhere.
He was almost ready to give up.

In the park, skaters danced across the frozen pond and children romped through the snow.

Just as Jack reached for
the kangaroo, a badger
bumped into him and
he fell to the ground.

Then in the distance Jack caught sight of the bouncing toy at the entrance to the park. Once again he gave chase.

Jack slipped and fell on the ice as he reached for the bounding kangaroo. Quickly he leapt up and began running harder than ever. He *had* to get that toy!

The snowball raced through the village streets.
It rolled and rolled until—*boom!*—it crashed into…

Jack looked up and saw the kangaroo disappearing into a huge snowball the children were rolling down the hill. The snowball grew and grew, heading straight for the village.

Jack nearly caught the kangaroo, but just then—*splat!*—snowballs filled the air.

…Ginger's house. She threw open the door. Buried deep in the pile of snow she spied a small patch of brown fur. She picked up the little kangaroo and read the attached card, which said *Happy holidays to Ginger, from her sweetie.*

Heartbroken that he'd lost the kangaroo, Jack made his way to Ginger's house to tell her that he did not have a Christmas present for her.

Jack was about to knock when the door flew open. "Thank you for your present," Ginger said, holding the kangaroo close to her heart. "It's just perfect."

Everyone was having fun at Ginger's Christmas party.
"Now I have something for you!" Ginger told Jack.
She held up a beautiful new red coat.

"This," said Jack, "is the perfect present."